John Bayley

Catalogue of a Series of Original Designs, Cartoons, and Drawings, by the Great Masters of the Italian Schools of Art

SALZWASSER
VERLAG

John Bayley

Catalogue of a Series of Original Designs, Cartoons, and Drawings, by the Great Masters of the Italian Schools of Art

Reprint of the original, first published in 1859.

1st Edition 2022 | ISBN: 978-3-37512-606-3

Verlag (Publisher): Salzwasser Verlag GmbH, Zeilweg 44, 60439 Frankfurt, Deutschland
Vertretungsberechtigt (Authorized to represent): E. Roepke, Zeilweg 44, 60439 Frankfurt, Deutschland
Druck (Print): Books on Demand GmbH, In de Tarpen 42, 22848 Norderstedt, Deutschland

CATALOGUE

OF A SERIES OF ORIGINAL

DESIGNS, CARTOONS, AND DRAWINGS,

BY THE

GREAT MASTERS

OF THE

ITALIAN SCHOOLS OF ART,

LIVING BETWEEN THE PERIODS OF

ITS RENAISSANCE, IN THE THIRTEENTH CENTURY,

AND THE COMMENCEMENT OF

ITS DECADENCE, ABOUT THE MIDDLE OF THE SIXTEENTH.

SELECTED FROM

A VERY NUMEROUS COLLECTION,

FORMED DURING MANY WINTERS' SOJOURN AND TRAVELS IN ITALY,

BY

JOHN BAYLEY, ESQ.,

FROM THE MOST NOTED CABINETS IN THAT COUNTRY.

PRINTED FOR PRIVATE DISTRIBUTION.

CHELTENHAM :
PRINTED BY HENRY DAVIES, MONTPELLIER LIBRARY.
MDCCCLIX.

INTRODUCTORY NOTICE.

This Collection of Drawings of the early Masters had its origin, many years ago, in the acquisition of a number of very rare and beautiful Works which formerly adorned the Cabinet of the Marquis Niccolini, who, in the last century, was one of the most distinguished connoisseurs and patrons of the Fine Arts in Italy.

The interest excited by the possession of these beautiful Designs naturally led to researches for more, and thus their acquirement became a prevailing study—an absorbing pursuit—and, in the course of fifteen or sixteen years, it resulted in an accumulation of from sixteen to twenty thousand Drawings.

Many of these were obtained by tracing out descendants of those eminent Artists in the various Towns in which they had chiefly lived, or pursued their studies; but the greater portion by far was procured from the Cabinets of eminent connoisseurs and collectors of these treasures in Italy in former times, as the Riccardi, Buonarotti, Rinuccini, Capponi, Guadagna and Piattoli, in Florence; from those of the Dukes of Modena and d'Alva, and the Marquis Antaldi; from the Altieri, Giustiniani, Albani, Ghigi, Borghese, Doria, and other Palaces in Rome; and from smaller private Collections in different parts of Central Italy, Lombardy, and Venice.

The purchase, however, of the Piattoli Collection, in 1844,

consisting of between five and six thousand Drawings and Studies, formed, perhaps, the most abundant source whence this selection has been made, especially as regards the Works of the early Florentine and Tuscan Masters. Unfortunately, however, a considerable portion of that Collection had been deposited in one of the lower apartments of a house near the Arno, and when the great flood occurred in the year above mentioned, many of these were injured or destroyed by that catastrophe.

The Piatoli family had been Artists, Amateurs, and Collectors for several generations ; and, in the last century, Signori Gaetano, and, after him, his son Giuseppe Piattoli, were Directors of the Royal and Imperial Academy of the Fine Arts in Florence, and, consequently, had superior advantages in forming such a Collection.

During the last four years the principal objects pursued towards this Collection have been selection, and, from time to time, to discard from it every Drawing that did not possess a high and material interest, either from its antiquity, its rarity, or its excellence. It has thus been reduced to about the twentieth part of its former numbers ; and the surplus has partly been disposed of in masses, and partly been given to Schools of Art.

* These were comprised in 16 folio volumes, layed on Italian Cartridge paper, arranged under the names of their respective authors, and classed in schools, with occasional notes written under them, particularly the most important, stating the sources whence they were obtained &c. — The larger drawings w.ch co.d not be conveniently placed in books, were likewise layed on Cartridge paper and similarly classified in portfolios: the state, however, in w.ch they were found after that unfortunate inundation rendered their removal from those paper backs indispensible; but the names of the authors & other particulars have been carefully preserved & followed.

x It is believed that there does not now exist
any drawing of that early period so per-
fect and so important as this.

* A study for one of his noted pictures in
Florence representing the wars between
the Florentines and the Pisans.

SELECTED DRAWINGS AND DESIGNS

OF THE

GREAT ITALIAN MASTERS.

VOLUME A,

BOUND IN RUSSIA LEATHER, WITH CLASPS AND METAL CORNERS,

CONTAINS

THE FOLLOWING WORKS.

GIOVANNI CIMABUE, FIORENTINO, 1240—1300.

THE DESTRUCTION OF DATHAN AND ABIRAM. About the centre of the Drawing, and in advance of their tents, the earth is swallowing them up. There are Groups of Figures on the right and left; and in front of the latter Moses kneels in the attitude of prayer, Aaron standing behind him. It is one of his subjects illustrating the Old Testament history, painted in fresco in the great Convent of S. Francesco di Assisi, a portion of which fresco still exists.[×] Pen and Indian ink, washed with sepia. 21½ inches long, by 10½ deep.—*folio 2.*

GIOTTO, FIORENTINO, 1276—1336, OR HIS IMMEDIATE SCHOOL.

A Group of Figures, some in the attitude of devotion, probably attending a sacrifice; drawn with a fine pen and Indian ink. Below, and apparently unconnected, is a study for a Female Figure, with a simple outline sketch of a vase or urn; and on the back are six studies of Figures admirably designed with pen, and washed with bistre. 9 in. high, by 6½ in. wide.—*fol. 3.*

MASOLINO DA PANICALE, FIORENTINO, 1378—1415.

AN ENCAMPMENT OF AN ARMY. In the middle distance, and on the right, are lofty tents. In front of the latter is a band of men in mail armour with long spears; and, towards the left, a large host, with banners flying, is marching out as if to battle.[×] Pen and Indian ink, slightly washed with sepia. 10 in. long, by 5½ in. deep.—*ibid.*

B

PERINUS PERUGINUS, 1390—1430.

THE NATIVITY OF CHRIST; the Shepherds and other Figures in adoration, and the Holy Father and Angels in clouds above. Designed with pen and Indian ink, washed with bistre, and relieved with white, on grey paper, signed P. Perugin. A drawing of great rarity and interest; but this master must not be confounded with Pietro Perugino, the instructor of Raffaelle. 12¼ in. high, by 8⅛ in. wide.—*fol.* 4.

BEATO GIOVANNI ANGELICO, DA FIESOLE, 1387—1455.

An Ecclesiastic holding a Book, with a circular inscription—BEATO GIOVANNI PRIORE—over his head. Black, relieved with white. 9¾ in. high, by 7 in. wide.—*fol.* 5.

A Female Figure, holding a garland in the right hand, and ears of corn in the left. Black and white chalks, on prepared paper. 10⅜ in. by 7 in.—*ibid.*

A Female Figure, drawn with Italian pencil or black chalk, from the antique. 11½ in. by 7 in.—*fol.* 6.

MASACCIO FIORENTINO, 1401—43.

LA DISPUTA, or Conference of the Doctors of the Church on the Sacrament. On prepared ground, beautifully drawn with bistre and relieved delicately with white. The Heads represent Pope Martin and other distinguished men. 7⅛ in. long by 4¾ in. deep.—*ib.*

THE SACRIFICE OF LYSTRA. Fine pen and Indian ink, the principal figures washed with *bleu de l'Inde* and relieved with white. 10¾ in. by 8⅛ in.—*fol.* 7.

Head of an Old Man, drawn with fine pen and Indian ink, on a prepared ground. 9¼ in. by 7½ in.—*ib.*

CHRIST'S ENTRY INTO JERUSALEM. Architecture and numerous Figures, drawn with Italian pencil on a prepared grey ground. Inscribed Mazzaccio Fiorentino. *See note on the back.* 13 in. by 11⅓ in.—*fol.* 8.

A portion of the Last Supper, consisting of part of the figure of our Saviour, with six of His Disciples on His right hand. Pen and Indian ink. 10¼ in. by 7½ in.—*fol.* 9.

FRA. FILIPPO LIPPI, FIORENTINO, 1400—1469.

THE MURDER OF THE INNOCENTS. This design exhibits great originality of thought and nothing of the usual mode of treating the subject. The scene is in a large hall of Herod's palace, adorned with statues. Raising himself on his couch of sickness, he is directing the murder of children, and behind are their mothers phrenzied and shrieking with agony. Bistre, relieved with white. 9⅜ in. by 8⅜ in.—*ib.*

× Early in the 15th century this rare artist was — a noted painter in fresco, & adorned many churches & palaces with his own works & gave designs for others, particularly at Verona & Mantua. He was also a famous painter in miniature, to which he appears to have devoted the latter portion of his life. This fine drawing is perhaps unique, and it possesses a peculiar feature which enhances its importance. An effulgence emanating from the Divine Infant illumines the whole subject — even to the clouds, the Deity & the angels. This sublime idea, therefore, which has been attributed to Coreggio, & claimed for other artists, evidently had its origin in a much earlier time, & possibly may be due to this rare artist — Peruginus.

Beato Giovanni Angelico da Fiesole.
1387 — 1455.

Mary Magdalen going to the Disciples to tell them of Christ's resurrection. — "Now when Jesus was risen early the first day of the week He appeared first to Mary Magdalen, — and she went and told them that had been with him, as they mourned & wept." — S. Mark XVI. 9-10. — An exquisitely beautiful & interesting design. She is entering a corridor leading to a chamber in which are nine of the disciples in mournful consultation — two being absent — perhaps indicating the journey to Emaus. There is great sublimity in the figures & expressions of the apostles, and the whole subject displays all that devoted feeling which so charmingly characterises the works of this celebrated artist. red chalk relieved with white. — 10¾ inches long by 7¾ deep.

B. Giovanni da Fiesole.

King David playing on the harp. — a procession in which are many figures, some with musical instruments, & one bears a censer burning incense. — red chalk relieved with white. — 10 inches by 6 inches.

* Under his common appellation "Lippo" his works are noted by Vasari, according to whom, Lanzi & others, he was a grandson of Giotto, his father Tomasso de Stephano having married Caterina Giotto's daughter. "Lippo" painted at Assisi, in the Campo Santo at Pisa, at Bologna, Arezzo, and in Florence many subjects of the Old and New Testaments, & Vasari applauds his works as surpassing those of Giotto.

Francesco Squarcione, di Padua
1394 – 1474.

The Sacrifice of Jacob. — He is before an altar in the attitude of prayer, his family standing behind him with the Holy Father in the clouds beholding them. Drawn with silver point, and slightly shaded with bistre. 8 inches by 6½ in.

Filippo Tomassino *x.*

~~BENOZZO GOZZOLI~~, FIORENTINO, ~~1400—1474,~~ *1354—1410.*

THE ISRAELITES DEPARTING FROM EGYPT. Design for one of his subjects illustrating the Old Testament history, painted in fresco at Pisa. Pen and Indian ink, washed with sepia. 16 in. long by 10¼ in. deep.—*fol.* 10.

SANDRO BOTTICELLI, 1437—1515.

A finished Study for the figure of the Virgin in Lord Northwick's picture—"The Virgin adoring the Infant Saviour." Coloured chalks. 12 in. by 8 in.—*fol.* 11. *Picture now in Lord Elcho's Collection.*

ANDREA MANTEGNA, 1430—1506.

The Coronation of a Pope. Architecture and many Figures. Pencil, on prepared ground, slightly relieved with white. 11½ in. by 8½ in.—*ib.*

DOMENICO GHIRLANDAIO, FIORENTINO, 1451—95.

Head of an Aged Man. A fine study, in red and white chalks. 8¼ in. by 7 in.—*fol.* 12.

ANDREA VERROCHIO, FIORENTINO, 1432—88.

A Group of Ten Figures, some of them bearing shields. A subject of Roman history? Fine pen and Indian ink. 10½ in. high, by 8 in. wide.—*ib.*

ANDREA SANTUCCI, DI SAN SAVINO, 1446—1510.

A Female Figure, on prepared blue ground, drawn with silver point and delicately relieved with white. 5 in. by 4 in.—*fol.* 13.

PIETRO PERUGINO, 1446—1524.

A Study for the Head of St. Peter, drawn with red chalk. 12 in. by 8½ in.—*ib.*

Study for the Head of another of the Apostles; perhaps St. Andrew. Red chalk. 11 in. by 8 in.—*fol.* 14.

An Altar-piece. St. John in the centre holding the Cross; below, on each side, a Saint with a book, and a Landscape in the back-ground. Bistre, relieved with white. 14 in. by 8¼ in.—*fol.* 15.

LIONARDO DA VINCI, 1452—1519.

THE HEAD OF SANTA ANNA, designed for the Picture so called, now in the Louvre. Red and white chalks. 11 in. by 8½ in.—*fol.* 16.

THE HOLY FAMILY, with Angels adoring the Infant Saviour: on prepared ground, with studies on the back in red chalk. 10½ in. by 8¼ in.—*fol.* 17.

Head of a Boy. Black chalk, on blue grey paper. 6¼ in. by 5¼ in. —*fol.* 18.

BERNARDINO LUINI, 1476—1530.

Two Virgins, one bearing a Sacramental cup, and the other carrying a book and a censer. Red chalk. 11 in. by 6½ in.—*fol.* 18.

MARIOTTO ALBERTINELLI, FIORENTINO, 1467—1512.

One of the Apostles with a book and pastoral staff. Italian pencil, or fine chalk. 12¾ in. by 7½ in.—*fol.* 19.

LORENZO DI CREDI, FIORENTINO, 1453—1536.

THE CORONATION OF THE VIRGIN. Design for Lord Overstone's Picture, exhibited at Manchester, beautifully executed in sepia. 10 in. by 8 in.—*fol.* 20.

FRANCESCO FRANCIA, BOLOGNESE, 1450—1512.

THE VIRGIN AND INFANT CHRIST. Design for Mr. Lee's Picture, No. 124, in Manchester Exhibition? Sepia. 8¾ in. by 5¾ in.—*ib.*

RAFFAELLINO DEL GARBO, FIORENTINO, 1466—1524.

MADONNA AND HOLY INFANT, in clouds surrounded by Angels, and below are two Saints looking up to them. Pen and sepia, relieved with white. 9½ in. by 6½ in.—*fol.* 21.

VIRGIN AND SAVIOUR, attended by two Female Saints. Drawn with sepia. 5¼ in. by 4 in.—*ib.*

RAFFAELLO SANZIO DI URBINO, 1483—1520. ✗

LA DISPUTA, OR, "THE ASSEMBLY OF THE DOCTORS OF THE CHURCH TO ESTABLISH THE VERITY OF THE EUCHARIST," designed with pen and Indian ink. On the back is another thought or study for the same subject, boldly sketched with pen. This was Raffaelle's first work painted in the Vatican by order of Pope Julius II., and, as Descamps observes, 'it sufficed to immortalize his name.' Drawn with Indian ink or sepia. 15¾ in. by 10⅔ in.—*fol.* 22.

THE TRANSFIGURATION. Raffaelle's *primo pensiero* for this his most celebrated Picture, drawn with wonderful power. Pen and Indian ink, washed with bistre. 17½ in. by 11½ in.—*fol.* 23.

THE SYBILS, beautifully drawn with Italian pencil. Painted in the Church of the Madonna del Popolo, at Rome. 12 in. by 9 in.—*fol.* 24.

A Study for a Female Head of extreme beauty. ✗ In red chalk, delicately relieved with white. 12¼ in. by 9¼ in.—*fol.* 25.

A Study for the Head of the Virgin in a Picture in the Escurial. In red chalks, delicately relieved. ✗ 8¼ in. by 6 in.—*fol.* 26.

Design for a portion of the Picture called "Joseph and Potiphar's wife." In red chalk. 10 in. by 8¾ in.—*ib.*

* This and following works of Raffaelle are chiefly from the Pistoli Collection.

* It may be confidently said that this inconceivably fine head is not surpassed by any drawing known to exist. It adorned the Medici Collection & was obtained from the late Marquis Riccardi.

× An exquisitely beautiful drawing.

^ Figure of the Apostle St. John, also painted in the Vatican, drawn with red chalk.

Two small Landscapes, in sepia, on one folio, and Studies of Two Angels on the back, with pen and wash. 11½ in. by 8½ in.—*fol.* 27.

A SACRIFICE, with a Study of a Child on the back. Pen and Indian ink, with slight wash. 10 in. by 7¼ in.—*ib.*

A Female Head looking upward as in prayer, beautifully designed in red and white chalks.ˣ 11 in. by 8 in.—*fol.* 28.

The Figure of an Apostle. Red chalk. 16¼ in. by 9 in.—*fol.* 29.

Another Apostle : both in the Vatican. 16½ in. by 8½ in.—*fol.* 30.

˄ THE LAST SUPPER, painted in the Vatican. Pen and Indian ink, slightly washed. 18 in. by 10¼ in.—*fol.* 31.

An Angel, drawn with pencil and delicately relieved with red and white. 9 in. by 6¼ in.—*fol.* 32.

An Angel, drawn with red chalks. 9½ in. by 7¼ in.—*ib.*

TWO BOYS CARRYING THE DISTAFF OF HERCULES. Fine pen and Indian ink. 7⅝ in. by 7½ in.—*fol.* 33.

THE ASSASSINATION OF JULIUS CÆSAR. On the back is a sketch of the Colosseum. Pen, washed with sepia. 14¼ in. by 9 in.—*ib.*

A Female Head, from the antique, exquisitely drawn with Italian pencil. 8¼ in. by 6½ in.—*fol.* 34.

A Study for the chief Female Figure in the *Transfiguration*, drawn with Italian pencil, delicately relieved. 7¼ in. by 4⅝ in.—*ib.*

A Study of a Nude Male Figure. Pen and Indian ink. 14⅜ in. by 6⅛ in.—*fol.* 35.

ÆNEAS CARRYING HIS FATHER, ANCHISES, FROM TROY. Drawn with pen and Indian ink. 10½ in. by 8 in.—*fol.* 36.

A Study for Two Groups of Figures, in one of which are two kings. Pen and Indian ink. 10 in. by 9¾ in.—*ib.*

An Angel, designed for a lunette. Pencil. 7 in. by 6¾ in.—*fol.* 37.

AN AVENGING ANGEL carrying a Spear. Drawn with Indian ink or bistre. 10½ in. by 8¼ in.—*ib.*

ROXANA OFFERING PRESENTS TO ALEXANDER? Design for a frieze, composed of numerous figures. Pen and sepia. 11 in. by 5 in.—*fol.* 38. *probably copy of a basso relievo antique*

Design for a Roman Galley, elaborately drawn with pen and sepia. 13 in. by 9¼ in.—*ib.*

HORATIUS COCLES COMBATTING THE ARMY OF PORSENNA. Pen and Indian ink, washed with bistre. 10¾ in. by 6 in.—*fol.* 39.

Roman Galleys embarking spoils or treasures. Pen and slight wash. On the back are arabesques, architectural designs and figures, exquisitely drawn with fine pen and Indian ink. 12 in. by 7½ in.—*ib.*

The Portrait of a Lady, said to be Raffaelle's sister, elaborately drawn in red chalk, delicately relieved. *(See note on the back.)* 13 in. by 10½ in.—*fol.* 40.

St. John the Evangelist, with an open book and the Cross. Sepia or bistre, slightly relieved. Engraved by Marcantonio. 8¼ in. by 6½ in.—*fol.* 41.

An Angel Driving Adam and Eve out of Paradise. Taken from Masaccio in the Brancacci Chapel, and engraved by Marcantonio? Pen and Indian ink, washed with sepia. 8 in. by 6 in.—*ib.*

MICHELANGIOLO BUONAROTTI, 1474—1563.*

Head of our Saviour; being part of a large cartoon for " Christ bearing the Cross." Black and white chalks. 10¾ in. by 9½ in.—*fol.* 42.

Design for a vase or tankard; and on the back, studies of figures for lunettes in the Sistine Chapel. Pen. 11¾ in. by 7½ in.—*ib.*

A Griffin. Pen and Indian ink. 9½ in. by 7½ in.—*fol.* 43.

Studies of hands, limbs, &c.; and on the back, a Madonna and Infant Christ, &c. Pen and ink. 11 in. by 8 in.—*ib.*

The Sybil Delphica; a grand study in pen and Indian ink, with slight wash. 16¼ in. high by 7 in. wide.—*fol.* 44.

Studies of Heads and Architecture. Pen and Indian ink. 4¾ in. by 4⅜ in.—*fol.* 45.

The Infant Hercules Sleeping on the Skin of a Lion. Pen and Indian ink. 9¾ in. by 7½ in.—*ib.*

A Falling Angel. Study for a Figure in his *Caduta degli Angioli.* Designed for the Sistine Chapel.* Pen and ink, washed with bistre. 9¼ in. by 7 in.—*fol.* 46.

* After Michelangiolo had finished the ceiling of the Sistine Chapel, he contemplated painting two grand subjects on its end walls, one of which was the *Fall of the Angels*, for which he made several studies; and in 1533, Pope Clement VII. commanded him to prepare a design for the *Giudizio Universale*, to occupy the west end over the Altar, while the *Caduta degli Angioli* was to be painted on the opposite end. He made studies, but no further progress. Clement died in 1534, and his successor, Paul III., anxious for its immediate accomplishment, honored Michaelangiolo with a visit, attended by ten Cardinals! to prevail upon him to execute the *Last Judgment.* This stupendous work, 54½ feet high by 43½ wide, occupied him more or less for six years. It was first opened to public view on Christmas Day, 1541. The *Caduta* was not painted, but several of his studies for it still exist, two of which are in this collection.

* This and following drawings by Mich-Ang.
were acquired by Sig. Piatoli from the Buonarotti family.

THE LAST JUDGMENT. Figures on Clouds, bearing a column, and below a Female Saint kneeling—both being studies for parts of this great work; the former in the group at the very top of the Picture, under the vaulting, on the right; and the latter being a design for the Virgin, making supplication to Christ for the sinners. Exquisitely drawn with pen, and washed with China ink. 7¼ in. by 5½ in.—*ib.*

Study for a Male and Female Figure conspicuous in the principal compartment of the *Last Judgment*, on the right and immediately under the group above-mentioned. Black chalk, highly finished. 12¾ in. high by 9 in. wide.—*fol.* 47.

A Group of Figures, also a study for a part of the *Last Judgment*. Italian chalk or pencil. 11¼ in. by 8½ in.—*fol.* 48.

THE VISION OF SAUL. Admirably designed with pen and Indian ink. On the back are fine anatomical studies. 12⅛ in. by 8 in.—*ib.*

Study for the Head of an Aged Man, and another on the back, in red chalk. 9¼ in. by 7¼ in.—*fol.* 49.

A Candelabrum, designed for St. Peters, at Rome, beautifully drawn with red chalk. 15¾ in. high by 8½ in. wide.—*fol.* 50.

MICHELANGIOLO, OR HIS SCHOOL, PERHAPS DAN. DI VOLTERRA.

A classic design for a frieze, probably taken from antique sculpture. Fugitives or captives driven by soldiers on horseback. Below is a triumphal procession. Fine pen and Indian ink. 11¼ in. by 8¼ in. —*fol.* 51.

A Royal Galley, and groups of classic Figures, either designed for portions of friezes, or taken from fragments of antique sculpture. On the back are vigorous sketches of a male figure, two small groups, &c. Fine pen. 11¼ in. by 8¼ in.—*ib.*

TIZIANO VECELLIO, DA CADORE, 1477—1576.

A Boy's Head. Drawn with Italian pencil on grey paper. 6¾ in. by 6¼ in.—*fol.* 52.

Study of a Female Head, *à la sanguine.* 11¼ in. by 8½ in.—*ib.*

MADONNA, INFANT SAVIOUR, AND ST. JOHN, drawn with red chalk. 5¾ in. by 5 in.—*fol.* 53.

Angelic Figures. Red, relieved with white. 8 in. by 6½ in.—*ib.*

Studies of a Child's Head, and of architectural ornaments on the back. 6¼ in. by 4¾ in.—*fol.* 54.

A Child's Head, *à la sanguine,* and studies of drapery on the back. 8⅝ in. by 6⅝ in.—*ib.*

Figures boldly drawn with pencil and red chalk, relieved with white. 14¼ in. by 9¼ in.—*fol.* 55.

GIORGIO BARBARELLI, DETTO IL GIORGIONE, 1467—1511.

The Three Disciples sleeping in the Garden of Gethsemane. Indian ink or bistre, tenderly relieved. 10½ in. by 8¾ in.—*fol.* 56.

ÆNEAS CARRYING HIS FATHER, ANCHISES, FROM TROY. Red chalk. 11in. by 8in.—*ib.*

ANTONIO ALLEGRI, DETTO IL COREGGIO, 1494—1534.

ONE OF THE SYBILS, with an open book before her, holds a pen in her right hand, and is attended by two Angels; designed for a lunette. Sepia, relieved with white, yellow, &c. On the back an architectural drawing. 11 in. by 11¼ in.—*fol.* 57.

THE HEAD OF OUR SAVIOUR. A sublime study, highly finished, on prepared ground. 11½ in. by 8 in.—*fol.* 58.

An Angel descending, holds a trumpet in the left hand and a wand in the right. Red chalks. 12¼ in. by 8 in.—*fol.* 59.

AN ANGEL OF PEACE holding an olive branch in the right hand, and pointing to heaven with the left. Drawn with black chalk, relieved with white. 11¾ in. by 8¼ in.—*fol.* 60.

THE VIRGIN, WITH THE HOLY INFANT ON HER LAP, a Female Saint, and an Angel offering Fruits, with Angioletti, &c., above. Sketched with a free pen and Indian ink. 8 in. by 6⅞ in.—*fol.* 61.

Architecture, &c., resting on which are two Angels with an open volume. Black chalk and pen, delicately relieved with white. 9¾ in. by 6¼ in.—*ib.*

An Angelic Figure, in black chalk, delicately relieved with white, on prepared paper, and a study on the back. 10¼ in. by 7 in.—*fol.* 62.

An Angel floating in the Air. Red chalks, slightly relieved. 13¼ in. by 9½ in.—*ib.*

THE HEAD OF OUR SAVIOUR, beautifully drawn with black and white chalks. 12¾ in. by 9 in.—*fol.* 63.

MADONNA AND INFANT SAVIOUR, WITH ST. CATHERINE, surrounded by Angels; a Saint kneeling below with other Angels. Design for a grand Altar-piece. Pen and Indian ink. 12 in. by 8¾ in.—*fol.* 64.

NEPTUNE AND OTHER FIGURES, designed for a plafond at Parma. Bistre, on grey blue paper. 16¼ in. by 10¾ in.—*fol.* 65.

Angels playing on Musical Instruments. Bistre. 13½ in. by 9½ in.—*ib.*

GAUDENZIO DI FERRARI, 1484—1550.

THE VIRGIN READING, and the Infant Christ and St. John supporting the book. Sepia, relieved with white. 7½ in. by 7 in.—*fol.* 66.

THE CROWNING OF CERES. Sepia, heightened with white. 9¾in. by 6⅞ in.—*fol.* 65.

FRANCESCO GRANACCI, FIORENTINO, 1477—1544.

THE VISION OF CONSTANTINE. Consisting of many figures beautifully designed in red chalk. 13½ in. by 10 in.—*fol.* 66.

ANDREA VANNUCCHI—DEL SARTO, 1488—1530.

THE VIRGIN, INFANT SAVIOUR, ELIZABETH, AND ST. JOHN: design for a Picture in the grand-ducal gallery at Florence. Sepia, 10¾ in. by 7¼ in.—*fol.* 67.

THE HOLY FAMILY: design for a picture also in the Pitti Palace. Black and white chalks. 12 in. by 10 in.—*fol.* 68.

A Male Figure, seated. Sepia. 6¾ in. by 5 in.—*fol.* 69.

Study for a Male Figure. Pen, washed with *Bleu de l'Inde*, relieved with white. 11 in. by 8⅓ in.—*ib.*

LA CARITA: a fine group, painted in the Chapel of the Scalza, at Florence. Sepia relieved. 11¾ in. by 7⅞ in.—*fol.* 70.

Two Figures and Sculpture. Sepia. 5¾ in. by 3⅓ in.—*ib.*

Study for two Female Figures kneeling. Red chalk. 7 in. by 5¾ in.—*fol.* 71.

An Angel bearing a Lamp: drawn with Indian ink and sepia. 10 in. by 7½ in.—*ib.*

ST. JOHN THE BAPTIST, grandly designed with Italian pencil or black chalk. 17 in. by 9½ in.—*fol.* 72.

JEPTHA AND HIS DAUGHTER? A finished study in red chalk. 12 in. by 7⅞ in.—*fol.* 73.

Figure of an Apostle. Black chalk. 8⅓ in. by 3¼ in.—*fol.* 74.

ST. JOHN THE BAPTIST, drawn with pencil, and an Angel in red chalk. 9¾ in. by 7 in.—*ib.*

GIULIO PIPPI, DETTO GUILIO ROMANO, 1492—1546.

THE HOLY FAMILY: design for one of the finest of his works in the Gallery of the Palazzo Pitti. Bistre, or Indian ink, relieved with white, on blue grey paper. 13 in. by 10¼ in.—*fol.* 75.

A Study for the Figure of St. Peter, with pen, Indian ink, and sepia. 8¼ in. by 6 in. Engraved by Marcantonio?—*fol.* 76.

A Boy or Angel carrying an ark or casket on his shoulders, with musical instruments and books lying behind him. Beautifully drawn in bistre, on blue grey paper. 6¾ in. by 4½ in.—*ib.*

c

Two Children—the Saviour and St. John?—pointing to the Cross represented in a glory above them. Pen, washed with sepia. 5 in. by 4 in.—*fol.* 77.

DAVID STRANGLING THE LION, drawn with pen, washed with sepia, and slightly relieved with white. 8 in. by 4½ in.—*ib.*

A Roman Warrior, designed with chalks. 9¼ in. by 7¾ in.—*fol.* 78.

Two Boys; one drawing a thorn from his toe, and the other holding a vine branch. Pen and Indian ink. 8⅝ in. by 7⅞ in.—*ib.*

One of the Vestal Virgins bearing a chalice or censer. Pen and Indian ink, her robe tinged with *bleu de l'Inde.* 11¾ in. by 7 in.—*fol.* 79.

An Angel, carrying the cross and banner, appearing to Saint Bruno in the Desert. Sepia, relieved with white, on prepared ground.—*fol.* 80.

A Subject of Roman History: a noble prisoner conducted by guards; six exquisitely fine figures. Pen and Indian ink, washed with sepia, and relieved with white on prepared ground.—*ib.*

Study for a Roman Warrior, on horseback, carrying a banner, painted in the Vatican. Pen, washed with bistre. 11½ in. by 9½ in.—*fol.* 81.

A Female Saint with her arms round a Corinthian column; beautifully designed with pen, washed with sepia, and relieved with white. 8½ in. 3½ in.—*fol.* 82.

Study for a Male Figure with a cap on, and on the back are Angels, &c. Pen and Indian ink. 10¾ in. by 7 in.—*ib.*

GIOVANNI DA UDINE, 1489—1561.

The Figure of a Boy amid a cluster of luxuriant foliage, beautifully drawn in sepia, heightened with white. 13½ in. by 8½ in.—*fol.* 83.

PIERINO DEL VAGA, FIORENTINO, 1500—47.

Study for a Frieze: Galleys crowded with men engaged in furious combat. Pen and wash. 13¾ in. by 4 in.—*fol.* 84.

Roman Galleys, with many Figures, beautifully designed for a frieze. Pen, Indian ink, and sepia. 17 in. by 4½ in.—*ib.*

CHRIST TEACHING, from the fishing boat on the Lake of Genesaret. Pen, washed with China ink. 15¾ in. by 10½ in.—*fol.* 85.

PIERO COSIMO, FIORENTINO, 1441—1521.

THE ADORATION OF THE SHEPHERDS.—Pen and Indian ink. 5¼ in. by 4¾ in.—*fol.* 86.

FRANCESCO FRANCIA, BOLOGNESE, OPERAVA CIRCA, 1480—1515.

Figure of one of the Apostles. Red chalk. 9¾ in. by 4 in.—*ib.*

MARIOTTO ALBERTINELLI, FIORENTINO, MORT. CIRCA, 1512. .

ONE OF THE VESTAL VIRGINS, with studies of heads on the back.
Red chalk. 12 in. by 8 in.—*fol.* 87.

RAFFAELLINO DEL GARBO, FIORENTINO, 1466—1524.

THE VIRGIN AND INFANT SAVIOUR, surrounded by Angels, and
St. John with four other Saints below. Drawn with a fine pen, sepia,
and bistre, relieved with white. 13 in. by 9 in.—*fol.* 88.

POLIDORO CALDARA, DA CARAVAGGIO, 1488—1543.

THE HOLY FAMILY. Pen, washed with bistre. 14 in. by 13 in.—
fol. 89.

Soldiers in Combat. Sepia. And on the back a Group of Figures,
in pen and Indian ink. 8¼ in. by 5½ in.—*fol.* 90.

An elegant study for a Frieze. A king with numerous attendants,
his charger, &c.; probably Alexander visiting Diogenes. Drawn with a
fine pen, washed, and relieved with white, 8½ in. by 5½ in.—*ib.*

A classic Frieze; many female figures in sorrowful procession,—
probably the Roman women going to the camp of Coriolanus, to implore
him to spare their city. Most likely drawn from a *basso relievo antiquo.*
Sepia, slightly washed. 13¼ in. by 8½ in.—*fol.* 91.

MATURINO DI FIRENSE? MORT. CIRCA, 1528.

A Sacrifice, and, on the back, another design, both with pen, washed
with sepia. Perhaps copied from antique sculpture, or it is a drawing
of an earlier period of art. 11 in. by 7¼ in.—*fol.* 92.

GIANNANTONIO RAZZI, DETTO IL˜SODOMA, 1479—1554.

THE DEATH OF MARY MAGDALEN, with two Angels attending
her. Pen, washed with sepia, and relieved with white. 16¼ in. by 11 in.
—*fol.* 93.

THE SAVIOUR TAKEN FROM THE CROSS. A composition of five
figures, beautifully designed with pen, slightly washed with sepia, and
delicately relieved. 13¼ in. by 11 in.—*fol.* 94.

Figure of a Saint. Chalks on prepared ground. 12¼ in. by 8 in.—
fol. 95.

CHRIST TAKEN FROM THE CROSS. A composition of seven figures,
drawn with pen and Indian ink. 9 in. by 7¾ in.—*ib.*

GIROLAMO DA SANTA CROCE, 1500—1549.

An Angel supporting the dead body of our Saviour. *A la sanguine.*
13½ in. by 8 in.—*fol.* 96.

VALERIO CORTE PAVESE, FIORIVA CIRCA, 1550.

MEDEA DESTROYING ·HER CHILDREN. Black and white chalks. 12 in. by 8½ in.—*fol.* 97.

BARTOLOMMEO GROSSI, PARMIGIANO, FIOR. CIR., 1450.

THE THREE MARIES? Sepia and white. 8¼ in. by 4 in.—*fol.* 98.

BERNARDINO PINTURICCHIO, DA PERUGIA, 1454—1513.

Study for the figure of Goliah. Black chalk. 10 in. by 5¼ in.—*ib.*

MARCANTONIO FRANCIABIGIO, FIORENTINO, 1483—152+.

THE MARRIAGE OF THE VIRGIN, painted in the Atrium of the Annunziata at Florence. Red chalk. 10 in. by 8½ in.—*fol.* 99.

DOMENICO PULIGO, FIORENTINO, 1475—1527.

THE HOLY FAMILY, beautifully drawn with chalks. 8½ in. by 6 in.—*ib.*

ANTONIO ALLEGRI (COREGGIO), 1494—1534.

Two Figures of Boys : a Study in red and white chalks. 11 in. by 8½ in.—*fol.* 100.

GIROLAMO MUZIANO, BRESCIANO, 1528—90.

CHRIST ORDERING THE DISTRIBUTION OF THE LOAVES to the Multitude. Pen, washed with bistre. 11¾ in. by 9½ in.—*fol.* 101.

THE SYROPHŒNICIAN WOMAN kneeling before Christ. Red chalks, delicately relieved. 10¼ in. by 8 in.—*fol.* 102.

GIOVANNI ANTONIO LICINO, DETTO IL PORDONONE, 1474—1540.

A Study for the Head of St. Francis, in black chalk, on blue grey paper. 11½ in. by 8½ in.—*fol.* 103.

Portrait of an aged man, perhaps designed for the Head of St. Peter. Black chalk on blue grey paper. On the back are two small figures, beautifully drawn, *à la sanguine.* 12 in. by 9 in.—*fol.* 104.

FRANCESCO MAZZUOLI, DETTO PARMIGIANINO, 1503—40.

MOSES BREAKING THE TABLES OF STONE. Elaborately drawn with fine pen and Indian ink, delicately washed with sepia and white relief. Has been engraved. 12¼ in. by 3¼ in.—*fol.* 105.

THE CORONATION OF THE VIRGIN, who is enthroned, with the Infant Saviour on her lap, surrounded with Saints and Angels. Pen andI ndian ink. 8½ in. by 7 in.—*fol.* 106.

× This marvellously fine drawing represents Fra.
Bartolommeo's friend & fellow monk the celebrated reformer Savonarolo, who, on the plea
of heresy, was barbarously burnt to death
.x.t. Florence in 1498. It is a study for the
portrait that he painted of that holy man,
as described by Vasari.

THE MARRIAGE OF ST. CATHERINE, with architecture and various small figures. Fine pen and Indian ink. 8½ in. by 4½ in.—*ib.*

FRA. BARTOLOMMEO DI S. MARCO, FIORENTINO, 1469—1517.

A Study for the Head of a Monk, ~~probably~~ Savonarolo, in red chalk, relieved with white. 11¼ in. by 7½ in.—*fol.* 107.

ANDREA SALAI, O SALAINO, SCOLARE DI LIONARDO DA VINCI.

The Figure of a Pope bearing a censer, à *la sanguine.* 10¼ in. by 7 in.—*fol.* 108.

MERCURY, designed in a sitting position, à *la sanguine.* 10½ in. by 8 in.—*fol.* 109.

BALDESSARE PERUZZI, DA SIENA, 1481—1536.

A Study of a Nude Female Figure, with a mantle hanging on her left arm. Pen and Indian ink. 7¼ in. by 4½ in.—*fol.* 110.

SAINT BRUNO IN THE DESERT, with two Angels attending him. Pen, Indian ink, and sepia; and, on the back, a figure from the antique, drawn with black chalk. 10¾ in. by 7¾ in.—*ib.*

ANDREA SCHIAVONE, 1522—1582.

THE VIRGIN AND INFANT SAVIOUR, drawn with red chalk. 7¾ in. by 6¼ in.—*fol.* 111.

THE VIRGIN, INFANT CHRIST, AND ST. JOHN. Pen, washed with Indian ink. 9¾ in. by 7 in.—*ib.*

RIDOLFO GHIRLANDAIO, FIORENTINO, 1485—1560.

A Female Head, beautifully drawn with red chalk. Pencil sketches on reverse. 8¼ in. by 5½ in.—*fol.* 112.

HEAD OF THE VIRGIN: black and red chalks. 8¼ in. by 6 in.—*ib.*

JACOPO PONTORMO, FIORENTINO, 1493—1558.

THE HEAD OF OUR SAVIOUR; a study in red chalk. 8½ in. by 6½ in.—*fol.* 113.

BELLIN BELLINI, FIORIVA CIRCA, 1500.

THE NATIVITY OF CHRIST, drawn with pen, washed with bistre, and slightly relieved with white. 10¼ in. by 9 in.—*ib.*

MICHELANGIOLO ANSELMI, PARMIGIANO, 1491—1554.

A Study for the Figure of one of the Apostles, in red and white chalks. 10 in. by 8 in.—*fol.* 114.

A similar Study for the Figure of a Saint: red and white chalks. 10 in. by 8½ in.—*fol.* 115.

BENVENUTO TISIO, DA GAROFOLO, 1481—1559.

THE VIRGIN AND INFANT CHRIST, designed in his later manner, with red chalk; and on the back is a Study for a Female Head. 7¼ in. by 6 in.—*fol.* 116.

ANTONIO BEGARELLI, DA MODENA, 1498—1565. ·

An elegant Female Figure: red chalk. 8¼ in. by 7 in.—*ib.*

BATTISTA NALDINI, FIORENTINO, 1537—1590.

THE MATER DOLOROSA? a Head drawn with great feeling; and on the back is a Study for another Head, both in red chalk. 13¼ in. by 9¼ in.—*fol.* 117.

JACOPO ROBUSTI, DETTO IL TINTORETTO, 1512—1594.

The Portrait of a Venetian Senator, drawn in black chalk, 5⅝ in. by 4½ in.—*ib.*

The Portrait of a Doge of Venice? beautifully drawn with pencil or black chalk. 6 in. by 5½ in. Another head on reverse.—*ib.*

THE ANGEL INTERPOSING AGAINST BALAAM: pen washed with Indian ink. 5¼ in. by 4 in.—*fol.* 119.

THE CIRCUMCISION OF CHRIST: design for his noted Picture in the Church of the Servites at Venice? Architecture and many figures, on tinted paper, with fine pen and Indian ink, washed with sepia. 11 in. by 8 in.—*ib.*

THE HOLY FAMILY, WITH SAINTS AND ANGELS. Enthroned above is the Infant Saviour wearing a Crown. On his left hand, rather below, is the Virgin; and on his right, Joseph, surrounded by Angels. Underneath, on the right, are St. Catherine and St. Lucia; in front, is St. Francis, and on the left a Bishop, both in the attitude of adoration. Designed for a grand Altar-piece at Venice, on blue paper, with pen, washed with bistre and Indian ink. 12¾ in. by 9¼ in.—*fol.* 120.

UGO DE' CARPI, FERRARESI, FIORIVA NEL, 1500.

CHRIST'S AGONY IN THE GARDEN OF GETHSEMANE.—On blue grey paper, drawn with pen and Indian ink, relieved with white. 6⅝ in. by 4½ in.—*fol.* 121.

GIROLAMO DE' CARPI, DA FERRARA, 1501—1569.

THE TRIUMPH OF CHRISTIANITY.—A Bishop treads on the neck of a Hindoo, and is teaching children out of the Holy Scriptures. Sepia, relieved with white. 11¼ in. by 10½ in.—*ib.*

Volume D.

A corresponding Folio Book bound in
Russia leather.

It contains the series of original drawings –
illustrating the Iliad & Odyssey of ~~the~~ Homer
& the Tragedies of Æschylus, from which the
works edited by Flaxman were engraved.

The late Lord Northwick often studied these
beautiful classic works with great interest,
considering them of the highest importance.

PELLIGRINO DA MODENA, OPERAVA 1509—23.

A highly finished Study of Heads, in red and white chalks. 11½ in. by 7 in.—*fol.* 122.

RAFFAELLINO DEL GARBO, 1466—1524.

A Sybil attended by an Angel, designed for a lunette. Red chalk. 13¼ in. by 6 in.—*fol.* 123.

RAFFAELLO SANZIO, DI URBINO, 1483—1520.

L'INCENDIO DEL BORGO. A considerable portion of Raffaelle's cartoon for this grand subject, painted, under his direction, in the Vatican, by Giulio Romano. It represents the Conflagration of the ancient Burgh of St. Peter, at Rome, in the time of Pope Leo IV. Pen, washed with sepia and Indian ink. 15¾ in. by 13½ in.—*fol.* 124.

SCUOLA DI MICHELANGIOLO—DANIELE DA VOLTERRA?

A numerous train of figures, followed by horsemen; perhaps the departure of the Israelites from Egypt. Below is the Abduction of the Sabine women. Designs for friezes, or, more probably, taken from the antique; and on the back are curious studies. Fine pen and Indian ink. 11⅞ in. by 8¼ in.—*fol.* 125.

Elegant galleys and various groups of figures, perhaps copied from fragments of classic sculpture. Pen and Indian ink. 11¼ in. by 8⅝ in.

FRANCESCO GRANACCI, FIORENTÌNO, 1477—1544.

Portrait of a Florentine Officer of State. Red and white chalks. 11 in. by 7½ in.—*fol.* 126.

VOLUME B.

A LARGE FOLIO BOOK, CORRESPONDING WITH VOLUME A,

FILLED WITH

SELECTED DRAWINGS BY THE GREAT MASTERS,

CHIEFLY BELONGING TO THE

SCHOOLS OF FLORENCE, PARMA, LOMBARDY, AND VENICE.

VOLUME C.

A SIMILAR BOOK, FILLED WITH SELECTED DRAWINGS,

BY THE

PRINCIPAL MASTERS OF THE SCHOOLS OF BOLOGNA, MODENA, &c.

CARTOONS AND LARGE SELECTED DRAWINGS,

MOUNTED, AND

ARRANGED IN PORTFOLIOS ACCORDING TO THEIR SIZES.

PORTFOLIO A.

SANDRO BOTTICELLI, FIORENTINO, 1437—1515.

A MARTYRDOM. Two Roman Christians bound, are drawn on a car by a yoke of Etrurian oxen; and the kind of death they were to suffer is shewn by a fiery caldron which accompanies them. The procession is passing through one of the streets of Rome attended by a centurion, and soldiers armed with spears; and hovering over the martyrs are angels pointing to heaven. Design for a fresco, painted in the Church of S. Benedetto at Pisa. Drawn with red and black chalks. 20 in. long by 13 in. deep.—1.

Giulio Romano - 1492—1546.
~~GUIDO ASPERTINI, BOLOGNESE, OPERAVA 1422~~.

A Combat between Roman and Sabine Warriors? A grand and spirited drawing in Indian ink and bistre, relieved with white. 22½ in. by 16 in.—2.

RAFFAELLO SANZIO DI URBINO, 1483—1520.

THE SACRIFICE OF LYSTRA? Many beautiful figures on the left before an altar in attitudes of devotion, and others standing behind them. Pen, Indian ink, and sepia. 22½ in. long by 8½ in. deep.—3.

MICHELANGIOLO BUONAROTTI, 1474—1563.

THE SCOURGING OF CHRIST. Noble architecture and numerous figures, beautifully drawn with Italian pencil or black chalk. 20 in. by 16 in.—4.

GIULIO PIPPI, ROMANO, 1492—1546.

THE CAPTURE OF CARTHAGE. The Romans, under the command of Scipio, are scaling the walls of the citadel. Design for a picture painted for the Duke of Mantua, engraved by Penz. It ¦passed thence into the Orleans Collection. Sepia, bistre, pen and Indian ink. Pen studies on the back. 22½ in. by 16½ in.—5.

* A fine impression of this engraving in the stock of Messrs Smith print-sellers sold by Messrs Sotheby & Co. realized 70 or 72 <del>guineas</del>.

a b c

These noble drawings may be classed among the finest works of Correggio known to exist.

* a most rare and important drawing in wonderfully fine preservation.

DANIELE RICCIERELLI DI VOLTERRA, 1500—1556.

THE HOLY COMMUNION. A Saint in Pontifical robes, is offering up the Sacred Wafer to the Saviour, who is represented in the centre, with the instruments and signs of His Cross and Passion on either side. Above are the Father and the Holy Spirit; and below, are bishops, and heads of the Church. Elaborately drawn with fine pen and Indian ink. 18¼ in by 14½ in.—6.

NICOLO DELL' ABATE, MODENESE, 1509—1571.

THE BAPTISM OF SAINT AUGUSTINE. Elegant buildings and figures, with landscape in the distance; drawn with pen, and washed with Indian ink or bistre. 22¼ in. by 15¼ in.—7.

ANGIOLO BRONZINO, FIORENTINO, 1502—1567.

THE LIFTING UP OF THE BRAZEN SERPENT. A multitude of figures in a landscape, Moses and Aaron standing in the centre—design for one of the Frescoes painted by him in the Chapel of the Palazzo Vecchio, at Florence, by order of the Duke, Cosmo de 'Medici, and particularly described by Vasari in his account of the Royal Academy of Design at Florence. Pen and Indian ink, washed with sepia. 21¼ in. by 16¼ in.—8.

ANTONIO ALLEGRI, DETTO IL COREGGIO, 1494—1534.

A CHOIR OF ANGELS. They are borne on clouds, with an open book and musical instruments; painted in the Church of San Giovanni, at Parma. Beautifully drawn with pen, washed with bistre, and relieved with white. 22 in. by 15½ in.—9.

b THE ALMIGHTY GLORIFYING THE SAVIOUR. The Holy Father in clouds is pointing to the Infant Christ, who is borne and surrounded by Angels below. Design for a grand Plafond, painted in the Church of San Giovanni at Parma. Italian pencil and black chalk. 23½ in. by 17 in.—10.

c THE VIRGIN, INFANT SAVIOUR, AND SAINT JOSEPH. The Holy Infant on the lap of the Virgin holds a lily; and on their right is St. Joseph, also holding a lily. They are represented in clouds surrounded with Angels, and below is a female Saint borne towards them by Angels. Design for a Plafond, also painted at Parma. Black Italian chalk, delicately relieved with white. 24¼ in. by 17 in.—11.

GIOVANNI BELLINI MORT. DOPO IL 1516.

THE NATIVITY OF CHRIST. The Divine Infant rests in a manger, the Virgin, Joseph, and four Angels attending on him. On the right are figures bringing presents—a basket of doves and a lamb—and the wise men are approaching on the left. Drawn with pen, and washed with Indian ink. 25 in. long by 14 in. deep.—12.

D

RAFFAELLO SANZIO DI URBINO, 1483—1520.

THE THREE GRACES AND CUPID. A superb Drawing in red chalk for this celebrated subject, painted by Raffaelle, as a lunette, in the Farnese Palace at Rome. On the back are two grand figures; one a chalk outline, and the other drawn with fine pen and Indian ink. 22 in. high by 16 in. wide.—13.

BERNARDINO GATTI—IL SOJARO—DI CREMONA, 1522—75.

THE VIRGIN ENTHRONED ON HIGH, WITH THE INFANT SAVIOUR. On her left is a Saint (Carlo Boromeo?). On the opposite side an Angel is bringing a garland of flowers. Angioletti hover above; and in the lower compartment are two Angels and four Female Saints. A grand design, à la sanguine, for an Altar-piece at Cremona. 24 in. high by 13 in. wide.—14.

PELLEGRINO DI TIBALDI? 1527—1591.

THE EMPEROR THEODOSIUS REPELLED FROM THE CATHEDRAL AT MILAN. The Archbishop with the Canons, standing beneath a grand portico, refuses admission to the excommunicated monarch. His charger and retinue are around, amid buildings of the noblest architecture. Pen, washed with bistre, and relieved with white. 23 in. high by 17 in. wide.—15.

GUILIO CAMPI, CREMONESE, 1500—1575.

THE VIRGIN, WITH THE HOLY INFANT. She is seated above, with a Female Saint kneeling beside them, and below are six other Saints in adoration. Red chalk, delicately relieved with white. On the back are two Studies of Figures, also in red chalk. 22 in. high by 17 in. wide.—17.

PAOLO CALIARI, VERONESE, 1530—1588.

THE MURDER OF THE INNOCENTS. A vigorous design, in black Italian chalks, relieved with white. 24 in. by 18 in.—18.

GUILIO PIPPI, ROMANO, 1494—1545.

THE NURSING OF JUPITER. A grand Study, in red chalks, for the picture formerly in the Orleans' Collection. 19¾ in. by 14¼ in.—19.

LIONARDO DA VINCI, 1452—1519.

THE INFANT SAVIOUR CARESSING ST. JOHN. Powerfully drawn with Italian black chalks. 22½ in. by 14¼ in.—20.

omissions &c

Giulio Romano. 1494 - 1546.

A very grand study of a head, drawn
with ~~with~~ great power.

*A most rare and beautiful design, adjudged
by the Baron Trichetti & other distinguished-
connoisseurs as one of the most sublime & —
valuable drawings of Lionardo extant.

PORTFOLIO B.

TITIANO VECELLIO, DA CADORE, 1477—1576.

THE HEAD OF AN AGED MAN, powerfully drawn with black and white Italian chalks. 13½ in. by 13½ in.—1.

MICHELANGELO BUONAROTTI, 1474—1563.

A NUDE FIGURE, seated under a tree, drawn with great vigour in Italian black chalk,—probably intended for Cain. 19½ in. high by 12½ in. wide.—2.

STATUE OF HERCULES, drawn from the antique with pen, finished with bistre, and relieved with white. 17 in. by 11 in.—3.

THE VIRGIN WITH THE INFANT SAVIOUR, who is lying on her lap, and St. John playing in a cradle at her feet: Study for a group in the Systine Chapel, on the left of the tablet bearing the names EZECHIAS, MANASSES, AMON, in the genealogy of Christ. On the reverse is a torso. Broad pen and Indian ink. 16½ in. by 11½ in.—4.

THE PROPHET JONAS AND TWO ANGELS: an incomparably fine study for one of the most noted of his groups in the Systine Chapel. Red chalks. 15½ in. by 11¾ in.—5.

ANTONIO ALLEGRI, DA COREGGIO, 1494—1534.

A FIGURE OF SAINT JOHN THE BAPTIST, drawn with red chalk, delicately relieved with white. 17 in. by 10 in.—6.

HEAD OF SAINT JOHN THE EVANGELIST: a sublime study, executed with red and white chalks. 16 in. by 11 in.—7.

ANDREA DEL SARTO, FIORENTINO, 1488—1530.

LA CARITA. Design for one of the beautiful works painted by him in the Chapel of the Scalza, at Florence. Red and white chalks. 17 in. by 12 in.—8.

MARCANTONIO FRANCIABIGIO, FIORENTINO, 1483—1524.

THE MAGDALEN WITH A BOOK, drawn à la sanguine, relieved with white. 16¼ in. by 12 in.—9.

ANTONIO BOSELLI, BERGAMESCO, NAT. CIRCA 1496.

A CHOIR OF ANGELS SINGING: an elegant design in black and white chalks. 15 in. by 14 in.—10.

FRANCESCO MAZZUOLI, PARMIGIANO, 1503—1540.

THE TOILETTE OF VENUS, ATTENDED BY THE THREE GRACES. Below are a bath, classic vases, and amorini. A beautiful composition, *à la sanguine.* 14 in. high by 10¼ in. wide.—11.

PAOLO CALIARI, VERONESE, 1528—1588.

MARY MAGDALEN ANOINTING THE SAVIOUR'S FEET. Design for a grand picture at Brescia, in the Monastery of Saint Nazare? Pen, washed with sepia. 17 in. by 11 in.—12.

BEATO ANGELICO DA FIESOLE, 1387—1455.

LA MADRE DOLOROSA. Design for a Fresco. Pen and Indian ink. 15 in. by 14½ in.—13. *a most interesting drawing.*

FRA, FILIPPO LIPPI, FIORENTINO, 1400—1469.

THE REPOSE OF THE HOLY FAMILY IN EGYPT. On the right, the Virgin is sitting under a palm tree with the Infant Saviour on her lap; Joseph towards the left, and behind him the ass is feeding, attended by an Angel. Angioletti above, one bearing a garland and another a palm branch, and there is an adoring Angel at Mary's feet. A landscape forms the distance. Design for Picture in Florentine Gallery. Pen, washed with Indian ink. 16¼ in. by 13½ in.—14.

ANDREA MANTEGNA, 1430—1506.

THE ADORATION OF THE MAGI. Noble figures, with landscape background. Drawn with pen, washed with sepia, and relieved with white. Picture in Florentine Gallery. 16 in. by 14 in.—15.

MICHELANGELO BUONAROTTI, 1474—1563.

THE FALLEN ANGELS. A group of demoniac figures cast on the earth. They are looking upwards in consternation, stricken with the terror of Divine vengeance. *(See note at page 6.)* On the back is a grand Study of a Nude Figure for the Systine Chapel. Red and white chalks. 19 in. by 14 in.—16,

RAFFAELLO SANZIO DI URBINO, 1483—1520.

THE EMPEROR CONSTANTINE DELIVERING THE CITY OF ROME TO THE PONTIFF. The interior of the Basilica, and a multitude of figures, beautifully drawn with fine pen and Indian ink. Painted in the Hall of Constantine, in the Vatican, by Giulio Romano. 21¼ in. hy 16½ in.—17.

L'INCENDIO DEL BORGO, or conflagration of the ancient burgh of St. Peter's at Rome, in the reign of Pope Leo IV., painted in the Vatican. Pen, washed with bistre. 16 in. by 13½ in.—18.

PORTFOLIO C.

BARTOLOMEO RAMENGHI, DETTO IL BAGNACAVALLO, 1484—1542. ♦

The Adoration of the Magi. Architecture and many figures, in red chalk, relieved with white. 23 in. by 16¼ in.—1.

TITIANO VECELLIO, DI CADORE, 1477—1576.

The Death of Marc Antony♦. Cleopatra and attendants bewailing him. Drawn with pen and Indian ink; and there are, on the back, vigorous studies of men in battle. 23¾ in. by 17 in.—2.

GIULIO PIPPI, ROMANO, 1492—1546.

The Siege of Troy—Troia Nuova: design for a Picture painted for the Duke of Mantua, subsequently purchased for the Orleans Collection. Pen and Indian ink, washed with sepia, and relieved. On the back is a Study of a warrior on horseback, with fine pen and Indian ink. Engraved by Bonasone. 20¾ in. by 16½ in.—3.

The Overthrow of the Giants: design for a Fresco painted in the Palace of the Duke of Mantua. Drawn with pen and bistre: formerly in King Charles the First's Collection. 18½ in. by 13¼ in.—4.

ANTONIO ALLEGRI, DETTO IL COREGGIO, 1494—1534.

The Eternal Father, represented in clouds, surrounded by a host of Angels. Design for a Fresco. Sepia, relieved with white. 24 in. by 12 in.—5.

S. Girolamo: a powerful study in black Italian chalks, being his *primo pensiero* for the celebrated Picture so called at Parma: on the other side is a finished Drawing in black chalk. 18 in. by 14 in.—7.

The Virgin Enthroned, with the Infant Christ; Saint George, with other Saints, and children, below. Study for his celebrated Picture, called the St. George, in Dresden Gallery. Pen and Indian ink, washed with sepia. 20¾ in. by 14½ in.—7.

GIO. ANT. LICINO, DETTO IL PORDONONE, 1474—1540.

The Scourging of Christ. Grandly designed with pen and Indian ink, washed with sepia, and relieved with white. *See note on the back.* 24¾ in. by 15¾ in.—7.

ANGIOLO BRONZINO, FIORENTINO, 1503—1567.

THE BAPTISM OF OUR SAVIOUR. Above are represented the Almighty and the Holy Spirit, and Angels standing on either side of Christ and Saint John. Sepia, tenderly relieved with white, 21 in. by 17½ in.

JACOPO ROBUSTI, TINTORETTO, 1512—1594.

THE LAST SUPPER. Powerfully drawn with bistre or Indian ink on blue grey paper. It departs from the conventional form—the Saviour and His Disciples being seated each on a stool, at an oval table. Painted in the Church of Saint Jervais, at Venice. On the back is a Study for a Nude Figure, and a spirited design with pen for another of his great works at Venice. 22 in. by 17½ in.—10.

ANDREA DEL SARTO, FIORENTINO, 1488—1530.

His own Portrait, drawn with pen and Indian ink. The marble Bust of this celebrated master, which is placed among his works in the Atrium of the Annunziata, at Florence, is said to have been chisselled from this Drawing, after Andrea's death. 16½ in. by 10¼ in.—11.

NICOLO PRIMATICCIO, NATO IN BOLOGNA 1490, MORT. CIRCA 1570.

THE PASSAGE OF THE RED SEA. The Israelites having closed their passage in safety, Moses is stretching out his rod, and the waters are returning and overwhelming the Egyptians. Pen and Indian ink. 17 in. by 12 in.—12.

IL ROSSO, FIORENTINO, 1498—1541.

AN ASSEMBLY OF THE GODS. An elegant design with pen and Indian ink, in the manner of Michelangelo. 16⅝ in. by 11 in.—13.

AMICO ASPERTINI, BOLOGNESE, 1474—1532.

THE PROCESSION TO CALVARY, CHRIST BEARING THE CROSS. A very curious design in sepia, bistre, &c., boldly relieved with white. 16 in. by 11 in.—14.

ANTONIO BADILE, VERONESE, 1480—1550.

THE HOLY FAMILY JOURNEYING INTO EGYPT. Joseph, with an anxious look and hastening step, is leading the ass, on which Mary carries the Holy Infant on her lap, and an Angel follows, offering to Him fruits. Pen and Indian ink, washed with bistre and relieved with white. 14¾ in. by 9¾ in.—15.

POLIDORO DA CARAVAGGIO, MORT. 1543.

A Triumphal Procession—perhaps that of Titus and Vespasian, painted in the Vatican. Below is another Study—a Combat of Roman Soldiers; both drawn with pen and Indian ink. 16¼ in. by 11¾ in.—16.

* Most probably a work of Mich. Ang. himself, obtained as it from the Buonarotti family.

** An inconceivably fine drawing, evidently a portrait.

** From the Marquis Riccardi's collection — formerly that of the Medici.

PORTFOLIO D.

MASACCIO, FIORENTINO, 1401—1443.

PORTRAIT OF POPE MARTIN. Black Italian chalk, slightly relieved with white, on prepared ground. 12¾ in. by 9 in.—1.

LIONARDO DA VINCI, 1452—1519.

A Female Head, exquisitely beautiful, drawn with Italian black chalks, relieved with white, on blue grey paper. 15¾ in. by 11¾ in.—2.

MICHEL-ANGIOLO, BUONAROTTI, 1474—1563.

A Head, powerfully drawn with pen and Indian ink, said to be a portrait of Savonarolo. 14½ in. by 10 in.—3.

A fragment of a grand design; a portion of his Cartoon for the *Battle of Pisa?* Black Italian chalk, relieved with white.—17⅜ in. by 7¼ in.—4.

FRA. BARTOLOMMEO DI SAN MARCO, 1469—1517.

Study of a Male Figure, executed with red chalk. 15 in. by 7¼ in.—5.

RAFFAELLO SANZIO, DI URBINO, 1483—1520.

LA GALATÆA : a finished Study for this elegant subject in the Farnese Palace, particularly noted by Vasari as having been painted entirely by Raffaelle's own hand. 10¾ in. by 9¼ in.—6.

A Group of Nude Figures in Combat, vigorously drawn with pen and Indian ink or bistre, on blue grey paper; being one of his Studies for the Battle of Ostia, painted in the Vatican. 16⅞ in; by 10¾ in.—7.

VENUS POINTING DOWNWARDS, attended by Cupid holding an arrow. Design for a Lunette in the Farnese Palace—see reverse. Red chalks. 10⅝ in. by 9⅜ in.—8.

HEAD OF POPE LEO X. A vigorous Study for the Portrait of his Holiness as he appears in the famous Picture in the Pitti Palace, holding a consultation with the two Cardinals Giulio de 'Medici and de 'Rossi. Italian black chalk on blue grey paper. 14¾ in. by 10¾ in.—9.

ROMAN GALLEYS, beautifully designed with fine pen and Indian ink. In the lower corner, on the right, is a wolf suckling the infant Jupiter. 20½ in. by 8 in.—10.

A FLYING CUPID with his bow: *à la sanguine.* 9½ in. by 7½ in.—11.

GIULIO ROMANO, 1492—1546.

An elaborate Study for a Vase or Urn. Pen and bistre, delicately relieved with white. 13 in. by 7 in.—12.

GIOVANNI DA UDINE, 1489—1561.

A grand design for a Frieze; composed of many nobly draped figures, apparently in consultation, some of whose heads shew a close affinity to Raffaelle, and on the ground between them are the eagle, lion, dog, and other animals. Bistre, relieved with white, on blue grey paper. 13½ in. by 10¼ in.—13.

POLIDORO CALDARA DÁ CARAVAGGIO, MORT. 1543.

APOLLO SLAYING THE CHILDREN OF NIOBE, being one of his subjects forming the history of Niobe painted in the Palazzo Buffulo, at Rome. Bleu de l'Inde and Indian ink, beautifully relieved with white. 15½ in. by 8¼ in.—14.

A classic design for a Frieze — Alexander receiving gifts from Roxana? Bistre and Indian ink, relieved with white. 10½ in. by 7¾ in.—15. *Taken from a basso relievo antique.*

JACOPO CARRUCCI DA PONTORMO, 1493—1552.

THE RAISING OF LAZARUS. This impressive scene is represented beneath a rock, with a multitude of figures admirably grouped and drawn. Chalks, relieved with white.—12½ in. by 8¼ in.—16.

A Figure sitting, and another Study on the back, both à la sanguine, relieved with white. 12¼ in by 8 in.—17.

CHRIST RAISING THE WIDOW'S SON, AT NAIN. "It came to pass that Jesus went into a city called Nain ; and as He came nigh to the gates of the city, behold there was a dead man carried out, the only son of his mother, and she was a widow." Grand architecture and scenery of the city form the back-ground. Drawn with black and white chalks. 15 in. by 10½ in.—18.

THE UNIVERSAL DELUGE, painted in the Church of St. Lorenzo. Bistre or Indian ink, on grey paper. 16 in. by 14 in.—19.

GIORGIO VASSARI, 1512—1574.

Figures of a Saint holding an open book, and Two Children. Sepia, relieved with white. On the back are Sketches of Limbs, &c., in red chalk. 16½ in. by 10½ in.—20.

Raffaello de Ubino.

A study for the portrait of an aged man
finely executed with black & red chalks

Michel-Ang. Buonarotti

A study for the figure of Hercules in a
sitting position, beautifully drawn with
red chalk.

Fra. Bartolommeo de San Marco.

A female head exquisitely beautiful and
expressing deep devotion. as likely It is the portrait
of Plautilla Nelli, a sister of the Convent
of St Catherine of Siena in Florence, who
was a distinguished artist and the in-
timate friend of Fra. Bartolommeo. He
left to her a large number of his precious
designs. These were afterwards bound in
two folio volumes, w.ᶜʰ remained in the
convent after Plautilla's death, till the dissolu-
tion of that house in 1812, when it's pro-
perty was sold. Eventually those trea-
sury came into the Collection of the late
Sir Tho.ˢ Lawrence, whence they passed
to that of the late King of Holland, &
are now in the possession H.R.H of the Duchess
of Saxe Weimar. They cost His Majesty 6000
gineas, tho' many of them were mere abstract
studies & sketches.

Mich: Ang: Buonarotti

Portrait of his friend and coadjutor,
Daniele de Volterra — a finished
study in red chalk.

x Most likely taken from a basso-relievo antiquo.

PORTFOLIO E.

LIONARDO DA VINCI, 1452—1519.

Female Heads: a Study in red chalks. 7 in. by 6 in.—1.

A Male Head, drawn with pen and Indian ink. 7 in. by 5½ in.—2.

MICHELANGIOLO BUONAROTTI, 1474—1563.

A Nude Male Figure, seated, designed for the Plafond of the Systine Chapel, in the angle over the Sybil LIBYOA: a beautiful Study in red chalks, with sketches on the back. Formerly in the collection of King Charles I. 15¼ in. by 11 in.—3.

Another Study for the same Figure, but in a reversed position: *à la sanguine.* 12¾ in. by 8 in. *Also in collection of King Charles I.*—4.

A cluster of Three Male Figures with arms raised, as for the support of a font or urn. An architectural Study, with fine pen and Indian ink. 11 in. by 7¼ in.—5.

Head of an aged Man, drawn with red chalks. 8 in. by 6 in. *Formerly in King Charles the First's collection.*—6.

POLIDORO CALDARA DA CARAVAGGIO, MORT: 1543.

MUTIUS SCÆVOLA BEFORE PORSENNA, holding his right hand in a flaming fire. Pen, washed with sepia and bistre, slightly relieved. Designed probably for a Frieze.ˣ 14 in. long by 8¼ in. deep.—7.

TITIANO VECELLIO, DA CADORE, 1477—1576.

THE PRESENTATION IN THE TEMPLE. A sublime composition, in bistre and Indian ink. 11¾ in. by 10¾ in.—8.

Head of an aged Man. A fine Study in black and white chalks. 9¾ in. by 7¾ in.—9.

ANTONIO ALLEGRI, COREGGIO, 1494—1534.

Angels playing on musical instruments: a sketch *en grisaille.* 13¼ in. by 9½ in.—10.

An Angelic Figure, in red chalks, relieved with white. 9¾ in. by 8¼ in.—11.

GIO. ANT. LICINO, IL PORDONONE, MORT. 1540.

HEAD OF SAINT SEBASTIAN. A finished Study in chalks, on blue grey paper: on the reverse is one of the Prophets writing, designed for a Lunette, also in Italian black chalk. 14¼ in. by 10 in.—12.

E

BENVENUTO TISIO, IL GAROFOLO, MORT. 1559.

A Female Head: an elegant Study, executed in red chalks, delicately relieved with white. 5 in. by 4½ in.—13.

A Female Head, very beautiful, drawn with red chalks, and delicately relieved. 11¼ in. by 9 in.—14.

FRANCESCO GRANACCI, FIORENTINO, 1477—1544.

A Female Figure, perhaps one of the Sybils, pointing with the right hand and holding an instrument in her left. A finished Study in red chalks. 15 in. high by 18 in. wide.—15.

PARIS BORDONE, TREVIGIANO, 1500—1570.

A Study for a Female Head, probably designed for Saint Cecilia, in black and white chalks on grey paper. 13 in. by 10 in.—16.

PELLEGRINO DA MODENA, MORT. 1523.

Figures of Two distinguished Romans, perhaps Emperors, in military costume, beautifully drawn with red chalks. 13 in. by 9 in.—17.

GIROLAMO MAZZUOLI, PARMIGIANO, MORT. 1580.

The Sacrifice of ~~Jacob~~ *Noah* A fine Study in pen, washed with sepia, bistre, Indian ink, &c. On reverse are Studies in pen and Indian ink. 15⅜ in. by 11¼ in.—18.

FILIPPO MAZZUOLI, IL BASTARUOLO, FERRARESE, 1496—1576.

A Female Figure, representing Justice. She holds a sword in her right hand, and a balance and scales in the left. Drawn with bistre, and slightly relieved with white. It is signed with his monogram, and on the back is the date 1546. 16⅜ in. by 10 in.—19.

JACOPO PALMA.

A Dying Saint, supported by Angels, is receiving the Holy Sacrament. Above are the Holy Father and Angels. An elegant composition, with fine pen, washed with Indian ink, and slight tinges of red. 15½ in. by 9½ in.—20.

GIROLAMO DE' CARPI, FERRARESE, 1501—1569.

THE BETRAYAL OF CHRIST IN THE GARDEN OF GETHSEMANE. A grand design, with fine pen, washed with sepia and bistre, and relieved with white. 15⅜ in. by 12¼ in.—21.

*Probably intended for Severus and his son Caracalla.

BATTISTA NALDINI, FIORENTINO, 1537—1590.

The Figure of a Saint, drawn with great feeling; probably a Study for the sorrowing Mother of Christ. Red chalks. 15 in. by 10½ in.—22.

THE ASCENSION OF CHRIST: a sublime Study à la sanguine. 17¾in. by 12 in.—23.

BONIFAZIO VERONESE, 1491—1553.

CHRIST DRIVING THE MONEY CHANGERS FROM THE TEMPLE. Architecture and many figures, drawn with pen on a yellowish ground, washed with sepia and relieved with white. 10 in. by 6¼ in.—24.

BARTOLOMMEO PASSAROTTI, MORT. 1592.

A Nude Male Figure, powerfully drawn with fine pen and Indian ink. 12 in. high by 7 in. wide.—25.

PAOLO CALIARI, VERONESE, 1538—1588.

THE WISE AND FOOLISH VIRGINS. An elegant Study in pen and Indian ink, slightly washed with bistre. 9 in. by 6¼ in.—26.

THE LAME BEGGAR at the Gate of the Temple called "the Beautiful." Design for a Cupola. Architecture and many figures, in pen and Indian ink. 17¼ in. by 9½ in.—27.

JACOPO ROBUSTI, TINTORETTO, 1512—1594.

THE ASCENSION OF THE VIRGIN, borne by a host of Angels, en grisaille. 12 in. by 8½ in.—28.

TAR. SALVI, DA SASSOFERRATO, OPERAVA 1573.

THE VIRGIN, WITH THE INFANT SAVIOUR, who is crowning a female Saint kneeling before him. A noble design in red chalks. 20 in. by 15¾ in.—29.

PORTFOLIO F.

LORENZO GHIBERTI, FIORENTINO, 1378—1455.

MARCUS QUINTUS CURTIUS on horseback leaping into the chasm of the Forum. Pen and bistre. 10½ by 7½ in.—1.

MUTIUS SCÆVOLA holding his right hand in fire before Porsenna. Companion subject. Designs for Sculpture in Metal, probably for panels in the doors of the Forum, or some other public building in Rome.—2.

SEBASTIANO DEL PIOMBO? 1485—1547.

THE RESURRECTION. Vigorously drawn with pen and washed with sepia. 13¾ in. by 10½ in.—3.

SCUOLA MILANESE?

PHAROAH'S DAUGHTER RECEIVING THE INFANT MOSES. An elegant design, in sepia relieved with white.ˣ 12 in. by 11 in.—4.

POLIDORO CALDARA, DA CARAVAGGIO, MORT. 1543.

A classic design for a Frieze. Indian ink and bistre, slightly relieved with white. 10¼ in. by 7¾.—5.

BACCIO BANDINELLI, FIORENTINO, 1487—1559.

HERCULES KILLING CACUS. Design for his famous Statue standing in front of the Palazzo Vecchio at Florence.* Drawn with Italian black chalk, washed with sepia and relieved with white. 15¼ in. by 8 in.—6.

MARCELLO VENUSTI, MANTOVANO, NAT. CIRCA 1488.

FAITH, HOPE, AND CHARITY. A classic group, beautifully drawn from the antique. Bistre, relieved with white. 12¼ in. by 9½ in.—7.

A Female Figure resting on a classic urn: à la sanguine, delicately relieved with white. 17¾ in. by 11 in.—8.

FREDERIGO BAROCCIO, DI URBINO, 1528—1612.

Portrait of a Lady, supposed to be a daughter of the Duke of Urbino, very delicately drawn with coloured chalks, on a fine paper with a very curious water-mark. 11¼ in. by 8 in.—9.

* When Michel-Angelo was employed by Leo X. at Carrara, procuring marble for the façade of S. Lorenzo, he selected a large block for a statue of Hercules killing Cacus, intending it to stand in the Piazza at Florence as a companion to his statue of David; and he made designs and models for that subject; but his time was subsequently so occupied by Clement VII. on works in honour of the Medici Family, that it was not executed; and Baccio Bandinelli obtained the marble, to form a similar composition, which he finally accomplished by order of the Pope, and this is his design for it.—*Duppa's Life of Michael-Angelo.*

* The highest perfection of art is displayed in this beautiful composition.

THE VIRGIN. A sublime head, drawn with Italian black chalk.
7 in. by 6½ in.—10.

FIGINO, MILANESE, SCOLARE DE LIONARDO DA VINCI.

THE ASCENT OF THE VIRGIN. In a circle surrounded by a host
of Angels and Seraphim. Below are Studies of Heads, &c., in the style
of Lionardo. Fine pen and Indian ink. 12¾ in. by 10 in.—11.

JACOPO ROBUSTI, TINTORETTO, 1512—1594.

CHRIST DRIVING THE MONEY-CHANGERS FROM THE TEMPLE.
Powerfully drawn with pen, and washed with Indian ink. Formerly in
the celebrated collection of M. Crozat, and subsequently in that of M.
Mariette. 9½ in. by 7¾ in.—12.

MURILLO.

ABRAHAM SENDING AWAY HAGAR AND ISHMAEL. A beautiful
Study, in black chalk, slightly relieved with white. 14½ in. by 10½ in.
—13.

BALDESSARE PERUZZI, 1481—1536.

THE PRESENTATION IN THE TEMPLE. Noble architecture, and
numerous figures, in bistre. 17 in. by 11 in.—14.

CHRIST GOING UP TO THE TEMPLE. A grand design, in pen and
Indian ink. 20¼ in. by 12½ in.—15.

BELLIN BELLINI? FIORIVA CIRC. 1500.

THE NATIVITY: an elegant Study, in pen and Indian ink, washed
with sepia. 18½ in. by 11¾ in.—16.

ALLESSANDRO BONVICINO—IL MORETTO, DA BRESCIA, MORT.
DOPO 1547.

A multitude of Saints looking up beholding the Father, Son and
Holy Spirit with Angels in the clouds. Pen, washed with bistre, and
relieved with white. 16¾ in. by 11 in.—17.

FRANCESCO TORBIDO—IL MORO, 1493—1549.

Martyrdom of one of the Apostles, perhaps St. James. An elegant
design with pen, washed with China ink. 18 in. by 10¾ in.—18.

MARCO DA PINO—SIMONE SENESE, MORT. 1578.

THE LAST SUPPER. Drawn with pen, washed with sepia, and
relieved with white, on a yellow ground. 18½ in. by 11¾ in.—19.

FREDERICO BAROCCIO NAT. 1528.

THE MURDER OF THE INNOCENTS. Architecture and a multitude
of figures, drawn in coloured chalks. 21½ in. by 14 in.—20.

PORTFOLIO G.

CARTOONS.

GIULIO PIPPI, ROMANO, 1492—1546.

TRIUMPH OF BACCHUS. Pen, washed with sepia, relieved with white. 25 in. long by 14¼ in. wide.—1.

THE FALL OF THE GIANTS. One of his Studies for this subject painted in the Ducal Palace at Mantua. Red chalks. 28 in. long by 15¾ in. wide.—2.

ACHILLES driving round the walls of Troy, and dragging the body of Hector, tied to his chariot. A grand Study à la sanguine for one of his subjects illustrating the Trojan war. 25¼ in. long by 17¼ in. deep.—3.

SEBASTIANO DEL PIOMBO, 1495—1547.

THE TITANS WARRING AGAINST JUPITER. Drawn with a fine pen and washed with Indian ink, slightly relieved with white. On reverse are various Studies in pencil. 25 in. high by 17¾ in. wide.—4.

GREGORIO PAGANI, NAT. 1558.

L'INVENZIONE DELLA CROCE. A grand Study in coloured chalks for this his most noted Picture. It was painted for the Church of the Carmine at Florence, and, with it, was destroyed by fire in 1771. 25 in. high by 18 in. wide.—5.

SCUOLA DI MICHELANGELO.—S. DEL PIOMBO?

MOSES STAYING THE PLAGUE OF THE SERPENTS, painted in the Church of Ogni Santi at Florence. Drawn with pen and sepia. 24¼ in. high by 18½ in. wide.

JACOPO ROBUSTI—IL TINTORETTO, 1512—1594.

The Crucifixion. An elaborate Study, with pen and Indian ink, for his famous Picture in the School of St. Roch, at Venice. 33 in. long by 18½ in. wide.—7.

An Allegorical Subject of many figures, designed for a Plafond. Indian ink, relieved with white. Autograph notes by Tintoretto surround the drawing. 22¼ in. by 16 in.

PAOLO CALIARI, VERONESE, NAT. 1528.

CORONATION OF THE VIRGIN. Design for this celebrated Picture at Venice. Drawn with pen, washed with bistre, and relieved with white. 26 in. high by 19 in. wide.—8.

× This design was by Mich. Ang. himself for a
picture in the Church of Ogni Santi at Florence.
It was sketched in outlines with pencil which
have been traced over with pen & Indian ink
probably by the artist employed to paint –
picture.

Michel-ang. Buonarotti.

A group of Figures probably designed for
sculpture, or a fresco painting. It is a
grand & powerful study in bold outline à la sanguine, 34 inches high by
21. inches wide. From the Buonarotti
collection.

* This very grand Cartoon has here been placed
under the name of P. del Vaga, that being —
written on the back of it in large modern
hand: but a very curious monogram in
the lower corner of it comprising all the letters
of MichaelAngelo's name, added to the gran-
deur of the design itself, leave but little if
any doubt of its being by the hand of Mi-
chel. Ang.

The Last Supper. A grand composition in sepia, relieved with white. 20¼ in. long by 9¾ in. deep.

SALVATOR ROSA.

The Crucifixion of Jesus Christ, on a Tree. A very noble Study, with pen, washed with sepia and bistre, slightly relieved. A multitude of figures, among which are the Holy Women at the foot of the Cross; and a bold rocky landscape forms the background. 29 in. long by 18¾ in. deep.—9.

LORENZO DI CREDI, MORT. 1531.

Virgin and Infant Saviour. A sublime Study for a Fresco. Italian black chalk. 29¾ in. high by 22 in. wide.—10.

MICHELANGELO BUONARUOTI, 1474—1563.

The Vision of Saul. One of his Studies for this subject painted in Fresco in the Paulina Chapel in the Vatican; a very vigorous design in pen and Indian ink. 32½ in. by 21½ in.—11.

Six Grand Cartoons or Studies of Angels and Children holding sashes or bands, designed for ornamenting a Cupola or Plafond. Pen and Indian ink, on grayish brown paper, and varying from 21 in. by 18 in. to 19 in. by 16 in.—Numbered from 12 to 17.

BACCIO BANDINELLI, 1487—1559.

Head of Hercules? A colossal Study in pen and Indian ink, probably for his celebrated Statue—Hercules killing Cacus—at Florence. 19 in. by 15¼ in.

PELLERINO DEL VAGA, MORT. 1547.

Jupiter Overthrowing the Titans. Above is a grand assembly of the Gods and Goddesses arranged on either side of the victor, many of which are represented in Portraits of distinguished persons of the time, among whom are those of several Princes and Princesses of the Medici. Below are the vanquished giants, some in defying attitudes. Washed with Indian ink. Painted in Fresco in the Doria Palace at Genoa. 47¼ in. long by 27½ in. deep.—18.

JACOPO BASSANO, 1510—1592.

Laban Searching for his Stolen Idols. An elaborate drawing with fine pen and Indian ink, delicately washed. A landscape forms the back-ground. 20¼ in. by 14 in.—19.

BERNARDINO LUINI, 1490—1535.

Two Angels, bearing a Crown between them. Part of a Design for a Fresco Painting of the Coronation of the Virgin: in Italian black chalks. 36 in. long by 18 in. deep.—20.

DRAWINGS AND CARTOONS, IN FRAMES.

DOMENICO GHIRLANDAJO, FIORENTINO, 1451—1495.

FRANS. ACOLTVS. A. IVRIS. CONS. A very fine Study in *tempera* for his head, preparatory to his painting an Altar-piece in the Acolti Chapel in the Church of Santa Trinita, at Florence, in which this celebrated lawyer, his wife, and nine children, are represented kneeling, and praying to the Virgin. It must have been painted prior to 1480, as he died in that year at a very advanced age. This beautiful and interesting Portrait, still in the purest state, was preserved in the Medici Collection, and was obtained from the late Marquis Riccardi at Florence. On panel. 16¾ in. by 11¾ in.—1.

RAFAELLO DI URBINO.

Study for the Portrait of one of the Princes of the House of Medici. Italian pencil, highly finished. This was also in the Medici Collection. 11 in. by 8½ in.—2.

THE TRANSFIGURATION. A finished design in sepia, relieved with white, for this celebrated Picture, probably the drawing prepared by Raffaelle for Marcantonio to engrave from. Having been folded in the middle, the upper part has broken off, and is, unfortunately, lost or decayed. 15 in. by 11 in.—From the Collection of Signore Giuseppe Piatoli, who, succeeding his father about the middle of the last century, was for many years Director of the Royal and Imperial Academy of Art at Florence.—3.

A noble Study for a Female Head, in Italian black chalks, relieved with white. Formerly in the Medici Collection. 15¾ in. by 10½ in.—4.

THE MURDER OF THE INNOCENTS.—Drawn with Italian black chalks, delicately relieved with white, probably to be engraved from. 16½ in. by 12½ in. Purchased in the Piatoli Collection.—5.

COREGGIO.

HEAD OF THE MAGDALEN. A grand Study in black and red chalks, relieved with white. 20 in. by 15 in.—6.

An Angelic Figure, beautifully designed in red and white chalks. 10¼ in. by 9¼ in. Formerly in the Collection of M. Mariette.—7.

TITIANO DE VECELLIO.

THE TRIUMPH OF CHRISTIANITY, represented by Christ, with the Cross in His right hand, treading down the dragon. Bistre. 15½ in. by 12 in.—8.

Michel-Ang. Buonarotti.

The apostles Peter & John restoring the lame man. — "A certain man lame from his mother's womb, was laid daily at the gate of the Temple wch is called "beautiful" to ask alms, who, seeing Peter & John about to go into the Temple, asked alms". — "Then Peter said silver & gold I have none; but such as I have give I thee". — This exquisitely fine composition represents on the left the celebrated gate of the Temple & act above noted, while on the right the Virgin is ascending to worship; & the subject is therefore called the "Santa Maria della Scala"; & is painted in the church of Sta Maria della Pace at Rome. — This splendid drawing is elaborately executed in sepia relieved delicately with white. — 24 inches long by 17 in. deep. — From the Buonarotti & Pistoli collections.

Lorenzo di Credi, 1453—1530.

A magnificent cartoon representing the Virgin Mary with the Infant Saviour. The figures display the highest standard of art & beauty, especially that of the Virgin. It is drawn with Italian chalk. 30 inches high by 22 inches wide.

33

LIONARDO DA VINCI.

The Nativity of "Christ the Lord."—"And she brought forth her first-born son, and wrapped him in swaddling clothes, and laid him in a manger, because there was no room for them in the inn."—"The shepherds said one to another, let us go even unto Bethlehem, and see this thing which the Lord hath made known unto us. And they came with haste, and found Mary and Joseph, and the babe lying in a manger." The scene of this beautiful and interesting composition is the stable of the Inn at Bethlehem, where Joseph is sitting beside the Virgin and the Divine Infant. God the Father, attended by Angels, is looking on them from above. The shepherds are approaching from the left, and a landcape opens on the right. Sepia, bistre, and Indian ink, heightened with white. 23 in. by 17 in.

ANDREA SALAINO, SCOLARE DI LIONARDO DA VINCI.

Lupa Receiving from Faustulus the Infants Romulus and Remus: designed for a Fresco painted in the palazzo of Prince Albani at Milan. Italian black chalks on prepared ground. 32 in. long by 24 in. deep.

BERNARDINO LUINI, SCOLARE DEL VINCI.

A Portrait of an Aged Nobleman; probably part of some grand historical composition for a Fresco Painting. Drawn with Italian black chalks on a prepared ground. 27 in. high by 19 in. wide.

BARTOLOMMEO RAMENGHI, 1484—1542.

The Adoration of the Shepherds: an elegant and noble Design, in red chalks, relieved with white. 25 in. by 18 in.

PIERINO DEL VAGA, 1500—1547.

The Titans Overthrown by Jupiter: a grand and elaborate Study for a *Fresco*, containing a multitude of figures, drawn with pen and washed with Indian ink. 50 in. long by 30 in. deep.

FREDERIGO BAROCCIO.

A sublime Study for the Angel in his celebrated Picture, *The Annunciation*, at Rome. Italian black chalk, relieved with white.

JACOPO ROBUSTI, IL TINTORETTO.

Il Paradiso: a Design for one of the most renowned of his works, painted in the Hall of the Grand Council at Venice. It comprehends an almost infinite number of figures, disposed with wonderful power and majesty. Drawn with fine pen and Indian ink on a yellowish prepared ground. 48 in. long by 24 in. deep.

F

THE CONSTRUCTION OF THE ARC OF THE COVENANT: a very grand composition, containing a multitude of figures, many bringing offerings in aid of the work. Moses is nobly conspicuous in the midst, and the building in a landscape forms the background. An elaborate Study for a *Fresco*, the figures especially being admirably disposed and drawn. Sepia and bistre, relieved with white. 5 ft. long by 2 ft. 8 inches deep.

FINIS.